KELLEE

"The Wizard Tells A Story™" Series Book #3

# The Secret Of GorBee Grotto!

## SECOND EDITION

© 1987 SCOTT E. SUTTON.

Written and Illustrated

## by Scott E. Sutton

# DEDICATION

This book is dedicated to the following artists who were of
great inspiration to me: Dr. Suess, Walt Disney, E.H. Shepard,
Holling Clancy Holling, Norman Rockwell, Andrew C. Wyeth,
Milton Caniff, Maxfield Parrish and J.R.R. Tolkien.

Thank you for making the world smile (and me, too.)

SECOND EDITION
FIRST EDITION 1987
SECOND EDITION 1990

## SPECIAL ACKNOWLEDGMENTS

I want to thank my wife Susie, Walt and Mary Conley,
Bill Runyon and L. Ron Hubbard for their help and encouragement.

## AUTHOR'S NOTE

Inspirations for the morals in this book are from the booklet *"The Way To Happiness,"*
a non-religious moral code based wholly on common sense. In 1984 I did some of the
illustrations (along with 16 other artists) for *"The Way To Happiness"* booklet.
I was so impressed with the workability of this moral code that I decided to use
the precepts as the basis for the morals in my books.

PUBLISHED BY

# SUTTON PUBLICATIONS, INC.

EDUCATION
THROUGH
IMAGINATION
TM

Irvine, California

Typesetting by Executive Design Group Enterprises, Santa Ana, CA
Printed in Hong Kong by South Sea International Press LTD., Seattle, WA
ISBN 0-9617199-3-1

Reading books is like digging up gold,
You get to have all the treasures they hold.

If you find a word you don't understand,
Ask a parent or teacher to give you a hand.

It may be hard and a little bit scary,
But learn to look up words in a **Dictionary**.

It's a book that tells you what words mean,
And it's one of the best books I've ever seen.

## The Planet of Ree

I'm going to tell you about a place,
Way out there, in outer space.
A planet whose colors are blue and green,
Sort of like pictures of Earth you've seen.

The planet's name is the Planet of Ree,
It's somewhere off in a blue galaxy.
It's a long, long way away from here,
Don't try to walk, you're nowhere near.
It's a magical place with millions of trees,
And twenty plus two fresh water seas.
It has two big moons up in the sky.
When you can't see one, the other goes by.

There are lots of great critters that live in this place,
On this Planet way out in outer space.
They're all different sizes, some as small as a mouse,
There are Sea Beasties and Dragons as big as a house.

The place is run by Wizards and Trees,
And a group of Sea Queens who care for the seas.
By themselves this work is too much for one,
But with many assistants they get it all done.

Ree wasn't always such a great place to stay,
A big disaster almost ate it away.
But all of its critters worked together, you see,
And solved Ree's big problem like a big family.

So have a good time as you go through this book,
At a brand new world you get to look.
You don't even have to leave your own room,
Just use imagination - take off and go ZOOM!

# WHO'S WHO ON THE PLANET REE

**BEEBEES**

On the Planet of Ree all talking trees,
Have hard working teams of helper BeeBees.
They live in the trees and keep them quite clean.
They're the best scouts and messengers a tree's ever seen.
At times they're mischievous but they're honest and true.
Without the round BeeBees what would a tree do?

**ERFS** (Wizard's Assistants)

These are Erfs. Did you know that?
They measure three feet from their shoes to their hat.
They're honest and smart, tough and persistent,
'Cause that's what it takes to be a Wizard's Assistant.
When Erfs grow up they don't go away,
They all grow up to be Wizards someday.

**GORBEES**

It is said that on the Planet of Ree,
When a tree drops an acorn into the sea,
Why, that is how GorBees come to be!
They look like fat little porpoises to me.
They help out the Sea Queens in Ree's blue seas,
The way the BeeBees do for Ree's Talking Trees.

**SEA BEASTIES**

Sea Beasties are like dragons that live in the sea.
They're ridden by Sea Queens on the oceans of Ree.
They can swim very deep, and they grow very long,
And when Sea Beasties talk, it sounds just like a song.

# WHO'S WHO ON THE PLANET REE

### SEA PRINCESSES

Sea Princesses help the Sea Queens get through
All of the sea work they have to do.
Such as watching the sea's Beasties and colorful fishes
And other sea critters such as Gorbees and Splishes.
As Sea Princesses grow up, eventually,
Sea Queens are what they will grow up to be.

### SEA QUEENS

Wizards take care of the land with the help of the trees,
And the Sea Queens take care of Ree's many blue seas.
The one hundred Sea Queens on the Planet of Ree,
Travel the oceans on their Sea Beasties.
Making sure that the sea critters are doing alright,
They work hard all day, sometimes into the night.

### TALKING TREES

All the trees on the Planet of Ree,
Have faces and talk like you and me.
They are very old and wise,
And grow to a very large size.
When a Wizard grows old on the Planet of Ree,
The Wizard doesn't die . . . he becomes a tree!

### WIZARDS

I'm a Wizard, as you can see.
I'm one of the Wizards in charge of Ree.
We're not very tall, only five feet two.
We have stars on our robes and our robes are all blue.
There are 100 Wizards on the Planet of Ree.
We're the wisest and kindest you'll ever see.

# The Secret Of Gorbee Grotto

1

It's another fine day on the Planet of Ree,
And if we look closely, what do we see?

Well, down in a clearing near the Wizard's place
There's Jeeter, the Erf, with a smile on his face.

He's running with BeeBees as fast as can be,
Kicking a BooJee ball towards a goal Tree.

BooJee ball, on Ree, is a popular game.
It's sort of like soccer, but not quite the same.

One team kicks the ball to the other team's Tree,
When you kick the soft ball it sounds like "BooJee."

"IIYEEE!" yelled out Jeeter as he booted the ball.
The other team tried to stop him, but he got past them all!

"BOOJEE SWISH" went the BooJee ball and "BOOJEE" once more,
As it hit the big goal Tree for the game's final score.

"YAHOO!" cheered a BeeBee. "We won that game.
We're two games to two, so in games we're the same."

"One more game," said a BeeBee, "to end off the day."
"I'd rather," said Jeeter, "go swim in GorBee Bay."

"Mr. Wizard," yelled Jeeter, "can I swim in the Bay?"
"Fine with me, go ahead!" the Wizard did say.

"Let's race to the water!" yelled out a BeeBee.
Off they ran like a flash to the edge of the sea.

They leaped off a small cliff and dived into the surf.
"SPLASH" in the water went the BeeBees and Erf.

They swam in the waves, they rode quite a few.
They were joined by some GorBees who rode the waves, too.

"Ahhhh," sighed Jeeter, "this water feels good."
They stayed in the water for as long as they could.

But the sun was setting, it was time to go.
They watched as the sunset made the clouds glow.

As they started to walk back from GorBee Bay,
Jeeter saw something strange.  "Look at that!" he did say.

"Look at what?" asked the BeeBees.  Jeeter pointed to where.
"In the Bay, at the back," he said, "right over there."

"It's a light," yelled a BeeBee.  "Right there, I can see.
It's coming from where GorBee Grotto would be!"

A BeeBee asked Jeeter, "What's a "Grotto" anyway?"
"It's a cave," he said.  "I explored it one day."

"There's a big river in the Grotto, that runs all the way through.
The Wizard and I sailed it in his sailboat, too!"

"Did you really?" asked a BeeBee.  "Where does it go?"
"We only sailed part way up it, so I don't really know."

"Let's go get the Wizard, then we'll find out
What that light in GorBee Grotto is really about."

Away from GorBee Bay, back through the tall trees,
Ran the Wizard's assistant and all the BeeBees.

When they got back to the cabin they yelled through the door.
The Wizard looked at them all and wondered, "What for?"

"WHOA!" laughed the Wizard. "One at a time, okay?"
So Jeeter told Wizard what they'd seen at GorBee Bay.

"Hmmmm.  A light in the Grotto, very strange," the Wizard said.
He grabbed a cloak to keep him warm and put his hat on his head.

They grabbed something to eat, some muffins and fruit,
"Back to GorBee Bay," said Wizard.  "Hurry up, let's scoot!"

The Wizard, Erf, and BeeBees ran through the bright moonlight,
All the way to GorBee Bay 'til Wizard's sailboat was in sight.

They piled in the sailboat.  It was quite a tight fit,
But they all found a place in the sailboat to sit.

There was no wind at all, but Wizard's have ways
Of making sailboats sail on very calm days.

9

"Off we go!" said the Wizard. "Soon we will see
Just what is behind this Grotto mystery."

They sailed away from the beach and into GorBee Bay.
"Look, there's the light!" Jeeter said. "Over that way."

"Ah hah!" said the Wizard. "I can see it all right."
And he steered the sailboat right for the light.

They sailed along until they got to where
The Grotto began, then proceeded with care.

"Shhhh," whispered Wizard. "We mustn't scare
Whatever it is that's hidden in there."

"Look," said a BeeBee, "that's what's causing the light."
A campfire," he said, as it came into sight.

11

"So it is," said the Wizard as he steered the boat to land.
They jumped out on the beach and walked across the sand.

"There's no one here now," whispered a BeeBee.
"But there was," said Jeeter. "Look, footprints, see?"

"I've never seen footprints like these," Jeeter said,
As he stared at the ground and scratched his head.

While Jeeter and the BeeBees were studying the ground,
The Wizard was in the dark scouting around.

Suddenly the Wizard looked up and said, "Hello!"
"Hello," said a voice outside the fire's glow.

"I am a Wizard," the Wizard said politely.
"An I am a Woodrat," the voice said lightly.

"Yes, I know," said the Wizard.  The voice asked, "How?"
"Oh, the Trees told me," said Wizard.  "Come with me now."

"Sit by the fire and meet my friends here."
They walked from the dark and as they came near,

Jeeter's eyes opened wide, as wide as could be.
This "Woodrat" person was NOT from Planet Ree!

He was a rat all right, but taller than Jeeter.
His clothes were neat, his fur even neater.

He wore baggy pants, a shirt and a vest,
And he looked very friendly, not like a pest.

He wore a hat with a feather up on his head.
"This is Jeeter, my assistant," the Wizard said.

Jeeter said, "Hello" and the BeeBees did, too.
"My name is Bipp," said the Woodrat. "How do you do?"

"So, Bipp," said the Wizard, "you're not from this place.
What brings you to this part of outer space?"

"Well," said Bipp, "I have come a long way
To ask if you would help us today."

"As you know," Bipp went on, "we're not from Ree,
But from a planet far across this galaxy."

"The Chief Woodrat," said Bipp, "has asked me to see
If he could meet with a Wizard from the Planet of Ree."

"All right," said the Wizard. "So it shall be.
Since I am a Wizard, he can meet with me."

"Douse the fire and load the boat!" is what the Wizard said.
They all squeezed in the Wizard's boat and went full speed ahead.

Up the river and through the Grotto, away from GorBee Bay.
It wasn't long before they sailed through the Grotto all the way.

Just then the sailboat sailed out upon a peaceful moonlit lake,
And of course, the Wizard knew just what course he had to take.

"How long," Bipp asked, "have you known we Woodrats were on Ree?"
"Yeah!" Jeeter said. "How come the Woodrats weren't introduced to me?"

"But they were," laughed Wizard. "Here's a Woodrat, right in front of you!
Bipp and his friends have been on Ree for just a day or two."

"So how," asked Jeeter, "did you Woodrats get all the way here?"
"You'll find out at camp," Bipp said. "We're getting very near."

A BeeBee climbed the sailboat's mast to see what he could see.
"I see campfires," he pointed out, "on the shore beneath that Tree!"

"Thank you, BeeBee," the Wizard said and steered the boat to land.
When they reached the shore Bipp jumped out and shook the Wizard's hand.

"Thanks," Bipp said. "I'll be back soon, then I will take you to
The Chief of all the Woodrats so he can meet with you."

As Bipp went off into the night the Wizard had to say,
"Jeeter, you have a frown on your face that will not go away."

"I know," moaned Jeeter, "but I don't see why the Rats came here.
Maybe we should make them leave or make them disappear."

"Well," said Wizard with a smile, "here's what I would do:
Try to treat the Woodrats as you'd like them to treat you."

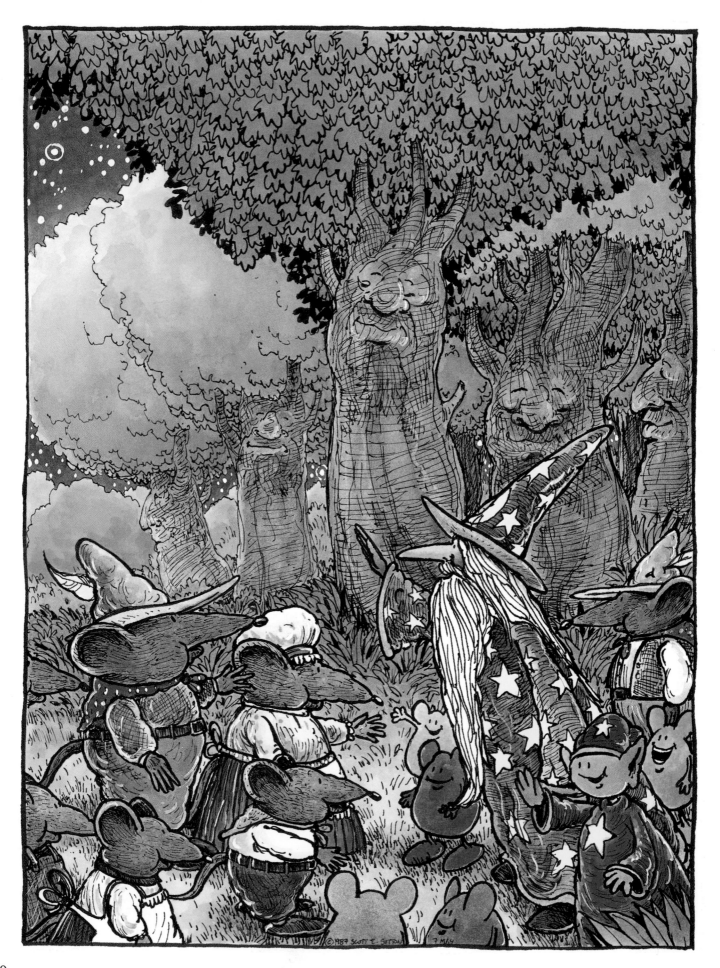

19

"Try," said the Wizard, "to see what it's like from the Woodrat's point of view."
"What if they mess up Ree," Jeeter asked. "Then what do we do?"

"Well," said Wizard, "what do you do when you have a doubt?"
"Look at all sides of the story," said Jeeter. "Then you can figure it out."

"Good!" said Wizard. "Let's do that now, then we will go from there.
When you find out all about Woodrats, they won't give you such a scare."

"Sounds good, Mr. Wizard," said Jeeter, as a smile showed up on his face.
Then from out of the shadows Bipp returned, walking a very fast pace.

"Let's go!" said Bipp. "Not a moment to lose. Chief Woodrat is ready to talk."
They got to their feet and started to run, because this was no time to walk!

When they reached the camp they were greeted by Woodrats of every size.
And noticed some strange looking animals. They couldn't believe their eyes!

20

At the center of camp was a campfire, around which they all sat,
Next to a white-haired old fellow who was the Chief Woodrat.

The Chief shook hands with the Wizard, both of them said "Hello."
"You've come to find out why we're here so now I'll let you know."

The old Woodrat was a kind being and spoke in a very calm voice,
"Our sudden arrival on Planet Ree was not by our own choice."

"I see," said the Wizard. "Well, Chief, tell your story to me,
Starting with this world of yours across our galaxy."

The Chief leaned back, looked up at the moon, and began to tell the tale.
"The world we're from was a beautiful place called the Planet Shale."

"We Woodrats were the forest rangers for many centuries,
Watching over all of Shale's critters, plants, and trees."

23

"But the sun that warmed our solar system just began to die,
Not making enough sunlight to light the daytime sky."

"As the sun burned out, the Planet Shale began to break apart.
There were snow storms and earthquakes and that was just the start."

"It was very clear to all of us that the end of Shale was nearing,
So I called the Woodrats and critters to a meeting in a clearing."

"Now, as you know, this galaxy is a magic universe.
Some people's magic is very strong and some a little worse."

"Our Woodrat magic is an ability we do not use a lot,
Unless we Woodrats find ourselves in a very dangerous spot."

"Well, as you know, and as I've said, we were in serious trouble.
We had to get off Planet Shale before it was space rubble."

"We formed a circle in the clearing standing close as close can be.
We knew the Planet Ree existed across our galaxy."

"We directed our attention to your planet out in space,
Then decided all at once to transfer to this place."

"In a flash we took off in a ball of speeding light,
Across the universe we zipped and got to Ree last night."

"As we left, I heard a noise, the planet shook and rumbled.
Just before we disappeared I saw it as it crumbled."

"And so you see we Woodrats just barely escaped from there.
Had we stayed on Planet Shale . . . well, the thought gives me a scare!"

The old Chief paused, looked upward and stared into the sky.
"That's how we Woodrats got here," he said with a long, sad sigh.

27

"But there's a happy part," the Wizard said, "that you forgot this night.
You saved yourselves and got to Ree.  Why, you made things go right!"

"Yes, that we did.  We made it here," the Chief said cheerfully.
"But still we need permission from you all to stay on Ree."

"Will you help us," asked the Chief, "get Planet Ree's okay?
We can do things to make this world a better place to stay."

"Like making cloth or growing food, useful things like that.
We'll help each other back and forth," said the old Woodrat.

"Of course, I'll help," the Wizard said.  "I think that you should stay.
I will get a meeting called and call it right away."

The Wizard called some BeeBees and called some GorBees, too.
He gave them each the message.  They knew just what to do.

The BeeBees ran and the GorBees swam off into the night.
With Wizard's message to be delivered to everyone in sight.

"Thank you, Mr. Wizard," Chief said. "Now I must get some rest.
If we're going to have this meeting soon I want to feel my best."

When Chief Woodrat went off to sleep, the Wizard went with Jeeter
On a tour of the Woodrat camp with Bipp as their tour leader.

They met almost all the Woodrats before the tour was through.
"There aren't many Woodrats," said Jeeter. "I counted eighty-two."

"There are eighty-four of us Woodrats on Planet Ree," Bipp said.
"Plus the critters we brought with us are over here straight ahead."

"Those big birds," said Bipp, "with long, long tails and legs
Are called Wallabean Grooses, and they provide us with eggs!"

MUPPIES

GRINGLES

WALLABEAN GROOSES

ZARTS

"Now, those round fuzzy critters that run around free
Are pets," said Bipp, "called Muppies, you see."

"That flying pod critter is what we call a Zart.
Even though Zarts are small those Zarts are quite smart."

"What are those?" asked Jeeter. "They look like BeeBees to me,
But instead they have horns where their ears should be."

"Those are the forest people of Planet Shale," Bipp said.
"They look like BeeBees, but we call them Gringles instead."

"Greetings!" yelled a Gringle with a very big smile.
They met all the Gringles and they talked for awhile.

There were twenty-two Gringles, from what Jeeter could see,
That made the long trip to the Planet of Ree.

33

"That's it," said Bipp, "now you've met everyone.
So let's get some sleep before the rise of the sun."

"Agreed," said Wizard. "I'm as tired as can be.
Jeeter and I can snooze beneath this old Tree."

"Goodnight then," said Bipp. "And thank you once more."
"No problem," said Wizard, "that's what friends are for."

Bipp gave each two blankets to make up a bed.
While making their beds, the Wizard then said,

"So, Jeeter, do these Woodrats still give you a scare?
Should they stay or should they go, what do you think is fair?"

"At first," Jeeter said, "I didn't want them on Ree.
But I wouldn't want that to happen to me."

"To lose my home and have no place to stay.
And they're good people, too. Let them stay, I say."

"I agree," replied Wizard, "they'll help us make Ree
An even better place to live for everybody."

As Jeeter and the Wizard fell asleep by the Tree,
The Wizard's messages were spreading fast all over Ree.

The BeeBees and GorBees told everyone in sight.
Then those critters told others.  This went on all night!

By morning Sea Queens and Wizards were rushing away
To get to the camp for the meeting that day.

The Wizards and Erfs arrived first.  They flew in,
As fast as they could, so the meeting could begin.

Then came the Sea Queens and Sea Princesses, too,
Riding big Sea Beasties from Ree's oceans of blue.

Now all of Ree's Talking Trees couldn't be at the talk,
Because Talking Trees have roots making it hard to walk.

But there were Talking Trees at the camp, much more than twenty.
They could represent Ree's Trees, because twenty was plenty.

Now all the people in charge of the Planet of Ree,
The Wizards, Talking Trees and Queens of the Sea,

Had arrived on time and were ready to go.
The Wizard said to Chief Woodrat, "Let's get on with the show."

The Wizard and Chief Woodrat stood on a  tall rock.
Wizard introduced Chief and Chief started his talk.

He told the scary story about the end of Planet Shale.
At parts of the story the crown turned pale.

As the Chief went on the crowd "oohed" and "aahed."
But (surprise) at the end the crowd did applaud.

They all jumped up and cheered very loud.
The Chief had never seen a happier crowd.

Then the Wizard got up and spoke to everyone,
"Now you've heard the story, here's what must be done."

"What the Woodrats need is a place to live,
And there is plenty of space on this Planet to give."

"So, all you Wizards, Sea Queens and Talking Trees,
Get together and meet, then start voting please."

The Wizards and Trees talked.  The Sea Queens did, too.
It wasn't long before the voting was through.

A Wizard and a Sea Queen shook hands with the Chief.
"You are welcome here," they said, to the Woodrat's relief.

Then one of the Trees spoke in a deep Tree voice,
"Of course they should stay.  It's the obvious choice!"

Well, no one was happier than the Woodrats that day.
"This calls for celebration," said the Chief, "right away!"

Everybody pitched in to make a big lunch,
Enough food and fruit juices to feed the whole bunch.

At the party some Woodrat children sang a melody
That they made up to sing to the people of Ree.

41

They climbed up on the rock, laughing and giggling,
And they sang this song while giggling and wiggling:

### WOODRAT SONG

Across the Stars, across the Stars!
Across the Stars we flew.

To Planet Ree, across the Stars,
A world we never knew.

Across the Stars, across the Stars!
Like lightning we went zappin'.

When we got here we were in fear,
We didn't know what would happen!

Across the Stars, across the Stars!
To a planet of green and blue.

We heard this was a wonderful place,
And what we heard was true.

Across the Stars, across the Stars!
To meet you people here.

And when we met you folks we saw
No reason for our fear.

Across the Stars, across the Stars!
Faster than a squeak.

Thank you all, you helped us out
When things looked really bleak!

Across the Stars, across the Stars!
Across the galaxy,

On Planet Ree we found a home,
Now we're happy as can be!

The Woodrat celebration ended later on that day.
Everyone else went home but four Wizards did stay.

To pick out a place on this part of Ree,
Where the Woodrats could settle comfortably.

43

Jeeter had an idea that he told them all,
"In those mountains over there I seem to recall"

"A big valley with a river and trees and flowers.
To walk there," Jeeter said, "only takes two hours."

"Why that's perfect!" said Wizard, and the others thought so.
"Jeeter and I will get them settled so you four can go."

"Fine with us," said four Wizards. They said their goodbyes
To everyone there, then flew to the skies,

Back to different parts of the planet of Ree,
As each Wizard has his own part of Ree to oversee.

"Okay, Chief, let's get to the valley," said Wizard.
So everyone packed everything as quick as a blizzard.

And as they all took off on the two hour walk,
The Wizard gave the Woodrats a very helpful talk

On important things about Ree to know,
Like how to fix the land so food will grow.

Or how to get wood by asking a Tree,
"Because all plants and trees are alive on Ree."

"And if you want something from them just make a request.
Just ask them politely and they'll do their best."

45

The Wizard told them Ree's history and how it was run,
And about all of it's critters before he was done.

Like Flying Floojies, Tree Gings, Snow Pookas and Splishes,
Dragons and Ploots, Sea Beasties and Fishes.

Sea Queens and Sea Princesses and Wizards, too,
And BeeBees and Erfs before he was through.

"We're getting close," said Jeeter, "just a short way to go."
They walked over a hill and saw the valley below.

"Oooh!" said the Woodrats.  They had to agree,
This was the perfect place for a Woodrat to be.

The Woodrats picked the best place in the valley to stay.
The Wizard told the Chief, "We'll fly in every day"

"To make sure you all are doing okay.
Now, Jeeter," said Wizard, "let's be on our way."

Then the Wizard commanded in a good Wizard voice,
"FLY JEETER AND ME TO THE PLACE OF MY CHOICE."

The Wizard and Jeeter flew out of sight,
Just before sundown when day becomes night.

They landed by the lake near the Wizard's sailboat,
And pushed it out from the shore so the boat would float.

The Wizard waved his hand. The boat zipped through the water,
Faster than a seal, a fish, or an otter.

Through the lake, through GorBee Grotto, and back to GorBee Bay.
"Well, Jeeter," said the Wizard, "we've had quite a day."

"No kidding," said Jeeter. "I'm glad that it's done,
But helping the Woodrats was sure lots of fun."

"You know," he went on, "I learned a new motto,
From this secret of GorBee Grotto."

"Oh," said the Wizard, "and what would that be?"
As he sailed the red sailboat in the blue sea.

"TRY TO TREAT OTHERS AS YOU'D LIKE THEM TO TREAT YOU,"
And you'll all do much better," said Jeeter, "if you do."

The Wizard was surprised. "well you can't beat that!"
He said, laughing so hard, almost losing his hat.

"Let's go home," said the Wizard, "and get something to eat."
"Good," said Jeeter, "then I can sleep, 'cause I'm beat."

Jeeter and the Wizard saw the Woodrats everyday,
And helped the Woodrats to get squared away.

Those Woodrats were smarter than anyone thought.
They built a whole town in two weeks, that's a lot!

They are great forest rangers and the greatest guides, too.
You never get lost when a Woodrat's with you.

So when Jeeter and Wizard go on a long trip,
They always go with their Woodrat friend, Bipp.

In fact, now, if Wizards have a big job to do,
They always ask for help from a Woodrat or two.

It wasn't very long before Woodrats came to be
A very valuable part of the Planet of Ree.

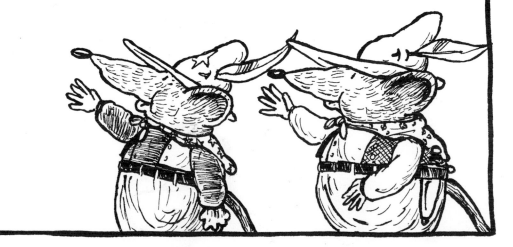

So now you are finished with Book Number Three,
Another great book about Planet Ree.

Well, I know something you'll like even more:
The Wizard Tells a Story™ Series, Book Number Four!

## Do You Have These
## "The Wizard Tells A Story"™ Series Books?

To get these books and other Family of Ree products,
send for your free catalog today!

Write to:
Sutton Publications
14252 Culver Drive, Suite A-644
Irvine, California 92714